D1021596

Zac's Bank Bust
published in 2009 by
Hardie Grant Egmont
Ground Floor, Building 1, 658 Church Street
Richmond, Victoria 3121, Australia
www.hardiegrantegmont.com.au

PEFC
PEFC/21-31-16

*The pages of this book are printed on paper derived
from forests promoting sustainable management.*

A CiP record for this title is available from the National Library of Australia

Text, illustration and design copyright © 2009 Hardie Grant Egmont

Printed in Australia by McPherson's Printing Group

3 5 7 9 10 8 6 4

ZAC'S BANK BUST

BY *H. I. LARRY*

ILLUSTRATIONS BY *ANDY HOOK,*
DAN MCDONALD, RON MONNIER
& ASH OSWALD

hardie grant EGMONT

CHAPTER...
...ONE

Zac Power was eating dinner. He was out with his mum and dad. He was having Chinese food.

His brother Leon wasn't there. He was busy. Zac was happy. He liked having his mum and dad to himself.

Zac was not an ordinary 12-year-old. He was a spy. He worked for a group called GIB.

His code name was
Agent Rock Star.

All Zac's family were
spies, too. They
worked to stop the
evil group called BIG.

And they went on really cool missions.

Zac's brother Leon was in charge of the GIB Test Labs. His spy name was Agent Tech Head.

AGENT / LEON POWER
CODE NAME / AGENT TECH HEAD
AGE / 14

He made the best spy
gadgets and vehicles.
And Zac was his test
driver.

Zac and his mum and
dad finished their
dinner. Then the waiter
gave them some
fortune cookies. Zac
took a cookie.

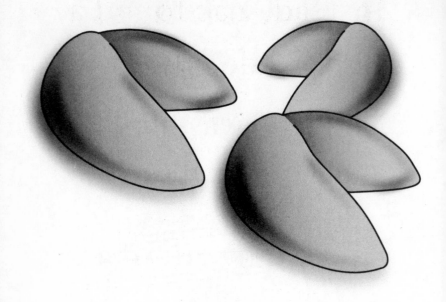

'I wonder what my message is?' said Zac.

But the cookie didn't have a message in it.

Instead, Zac found a disk inside. His spy senses were on alert.

It was a disk from GIB.

Zac put the disk into his SpyPad.

Every GIB agent had a SpyPad. It was a mobile phone and a computer. And it had the most awesome games.

A message popped up on Zac's SpyPad.

Agent Rock Star, you are needed urgently at the Test Labs. Leave through the kitchen door.

CHAPTER... ...TWO

Zac walked through the restaurant kitchen. It was very busy in there. People were cooking and putting food on plates.

There were pots and pans hanging from hooks. Zac didn't know where to go. Zac saw the waiter.

'Come this way please, Agent Rock Star,' said the waiter. 'I'm Agent Kitchen Hand. Did you like the way

you got your spy disk?'

'How did you put it in the cookie?' asked Zac.

'I'm not allowed to tell you that, Agent Rock Star,' said Agent Kitchen Hand. 'My jobs are top secret – just like yours. **Hurry!** Your brother

Agent Tech Head needs you.'

Then he took Zac through the back door of the kitchen.

Zac stepped out into a small lane.

'Agent Tech Head has sent a car for you,' said Agent Kitchen Hand.

The car looked like an old bomb.

Zac looked at Agent Kitchen Hand.

'You can't mean that old rust bucket?' asked Zac. 'My brother wants me to get into THAT? He's mad!'

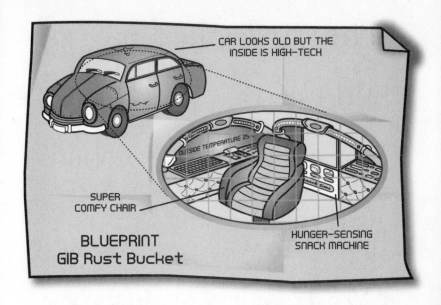

CAR LOOKS OLD BUT THE
INSIDE IS HIGH-TECH

OUTSIDE TEMPERATURE 25

SUPER
COMFY CHAIR

HUNGER-SENSING
SNACK MACHINE

BLUEPRINT
GIB Rust Bucket

'This is the GIB Rust
Bucket,' said Agent
Kitchen Hand. 'Please
get in. There is work
to be done.'

Then he went back
inside.

Zac looked at the car.
Its paint was peeling off.
It had rust everywhere.
And there were dents
in the doors. The wheels
looked like they were
about to fall off.

I wish Leon had sent a cooler car, thought Zac.

Zac opened the Rust Bucket's door. His mouth fell open.

'Awesome!' said Zac as he looked around.

The inside of the car was totally high-tech!

17

There was no driver
and no steering
wheel. There was a
computer instead.
On the computer
screen were three
buttons.

GAMES AND MOVIES
AUTO-DRIVE
SPY STUFF

Sweet, thought Zac.
And then he jumped.
Someone was sitting
in the back seat.
It was his brother,
Leon.

'Hi, Leon,' said Zac.

'Hi,' said Leon. 'I
fooled you, didn't I?

You thought this car was an old bomb! I need you to test drive it.'

'Cool,' said Zac.

CHAPTER... ...THREE

Leon showed Zac how to work the Rust Bucket's computer.

'This car knows everything,' said Leon.

Just then Zac's
SpyPad beeped.

BEEP-BEEP-BEEP
BEEP-BEEP-BEEP
BEEP-BEEP-BEEP
BEEP-BEEP-BEEP

It was a mission
from GIB.

Zac read the screen.

TOP SECRET
FOR THE EYES OF
ZAC POWER ONLY

MISSION SENT
THURSDAY 7.30PM

Someone is stealing money
from banks' cash machines.
You have to stop them.
Test drive the
Rust Bucket and
the Marble Flares
on this mission.

END

'The Rust Bucket will drive you straight to your mission,' said Leon. 'It will even tell you how to do your mission.'

'Very cool,' said Zac. 'And I can play games and watch movies while it drives!'

'Only if you have time,' said Leon. 'I need you to test drive some marble flares, too.'

Leon handed Zac a
box of chocolates.
Or at least that's
what it looked
like. But instead of
chocolates, there were
marbles inside.

There were
instructions stuck to
the lid of the box.

INSTRUCTIONS

1. Put on Marble Flare Goggles.
2. Throw Marble Flare at the ground. The flare will shatter. There will be a blinding light as bright as the sun. It will make the target blind for one minute.

'Marble Flares?' said Zac. 'These sound cool.'

'Follow the
instructions,'
said Leon.
'The goggles are
on the dashboard.
Good luck with your
mission. And don't
forget to do your test
drive report.'

Zac groaned. He hated
doing reports.
He just liked to test
drive gadgets.

He turned to Leon to
speak. But Leon had
already left.

On the screen, Zac
chose a movie to
watch.

Then he looked in
the back seat.

There was a snack
machine there.
Sweet! thought Zac.
*A machine with free
snacks and drinks.*

CHAPTER... ...FOUR

Suddenly Zac heard a voice.

'Please sit back and relax, Agent Rock Star,' said the voice.

'Enjoy the movie.
Help yourself to
the snack machine.
We will be at your
mission shortly.'

SNACK TIME

33

Then the car drove off by itself. It knew exactly where to go.

Zac was enjoying the movie. Everything was perfect. He munched on yummy snacks. But all of a sudden, the movie screen went black.

Zac groaned.
Right at the best part!
he thought.

Then the Rust Bucket
began to speak again.
'We will be at the
cash machine shortly,'
it said. 'Please look
at the screen,
Agent Rock Star.'

The screen started showing another movie. Then Zac saw that it wasn't a movie. It was real! He was watching a tape of two people at a cash machine.

'Those people look evil,' said Zac. 'Are they BIG agents?'

'Yes,' the car replied.
'Two BIG agents.
They are stealing from
the bank. Those bags
are already filled with
money.'

Then Zac heard a
noise. The computer
was making a phone
call. Leon answered.
His voice filled the car.

'Zac, BIG has made a
special bank card,' said
Leon. 'It works at any
bank's cash machine.
It lets BIG steal all the

money from the bank.
You must destroy the
bank card.'

'There are two BIG
agents,' said Zac.
'This might get
tricky.'

41

'Don't forget about the Marble Flares,' said Leon. 'They'll come in handy.' Then he hung up.

CHAPTER... ...FIVE

The Rust Bucket pulled up at the cash machine. The car was such an old bomb that the BIG agents ignored it.

They were still
stealing money.

'Please use the Marble
Flare Goggles, Agent
Rock Star,' said the
car computer.

Zac put the goggles on
and pushed the button
for the car window.
It slid down silently.

Then Zac threw two
Marble Flares at the
ground. They shattered
right at the BIG agents'
feet. There was a huge
flash of light.

The BIG agents
couldn't see! They
stumbled about.
They were both
rubbing their eyes.

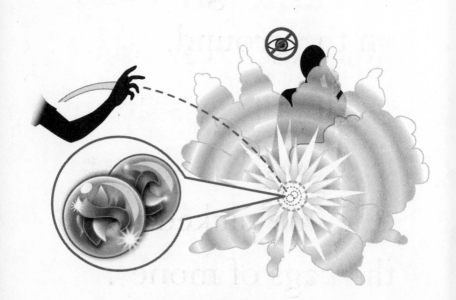

Zac only had a few seconds. He jumped out of the car.

The BIG agents were rolling around on the ground.

Zac quickly tied them up with rope. Then he picked up the bags of money.

Just then he saw a
melted bank card.
It said BIG on it.

*The marble flares
have melted the card,*
thought Zac. *Yes!
Mission finished.*

CHAPTER... ...SIX

Zac climbed back inside the Rust Bucket. He put the bags of money on the seat beside him.

'I'd better tell GIB about the BIG agents,' said Zac.

The Rust Bucket said, 'Calling GIB now, Agent Rock Star.'

Zac heard a click.

Agent Kitchen Hand's voice filled the car. 'Good evening, Agent Rock Star,' he said. 'Please come back to the Chinese restaurant now. GIB will collect the BIG agents. And well done.'

'Thanks,' said Zac.
'I'll be there soon.'
Zac clicked on
Games and Movies.

He picked his
favourite game to
play.

Sweet! thought Zac.
Now, time for a snack.

53

Suddenly Zac's
SpyPad beeped.

BEEP-BEEP-BEEP
BEEP-BEEP-BEEP

It was a message from
Leon.

Forget about
the snacks.
Where is your
test drive
report?

Zac groaned.
He wanted food
before he wrote
his report!

*I can't wait to get back
to the restaurant,* he
thought. *Maybe there
will be some fortune
cookies left.*

TEST DRIVE
REPORT

RUST BUCKET
Rating:

A car that can talk and drive itself is very cool! And the snack machine is awesome.

MARBLE FLARES
Rating:

These were great. I couldn't have stopped the BIG agents without them. I just wished they worked for longer. I had to be quick to tie the agents up!

END

... THE END ...